This Little Princess

story belongs to

· · · · · · · · · · · · · · · · ·

This paperback edition first published in 2013 by Andersen Press Ltd.
First published in Great Britain in 2012 by Andersen Press Ltd.,
20 Vauxhall Bridge Road, London SW1V 2SA.
Published in Australia by Random House Australia Pty.,
Level 3, 100 Pacific Highway, North Sydney, NSW 2060.
Text and illustration copyright © Tony Ross, 2012
The rights of Tony Ross to be identified as the author and illustrator
of this work have been asserted by him in accordance with
the Copyright, Designs and Patents Act, 1988.
All rights reserved.
Colour separated in Switzerland by Photolitho AG, Zürich.
Printed and bound in Singapore by Tien Wah Press.
Tony Ross has used pen, ink and watercolour in this book.

10   9   8   7   6   5   4   3   2   1

British Library Cataloguing in Publication Data available.
ISBN 978 1 84939 474 1 (Trade Paperback edition)
ISBN 978 1 84939 475 8 (Book People edition)

This book was printed on acid-free paper

A Little Princess Story

I Want to Win!

Tony Ross

Andersen Press

The Little Princess liked to win.

At the castle sports day, she entered the running race.

But after just a few metres she was out of puff.

"Stop!" she commanded the other runners.

"The race must be run in the opposite direction!"

Then she turned round and sprinted back to the start line.
"I've won!" she cried.

"I want to win!" she said when she played games at home,
and since everyone lost on purpose, she usually did.

But at school it was different.
There were cups there for everything . . .

. . . and the Little Princess wanted to win them all!

She tried her HARDEST at numbers,

but her cousin won the Numbers Cup.

She tried her HARDEST at painting,

but Polly won the Painting Cup.

She tried her HARDEST at writing her poem,

but Poppy won the Poem Cup.

She tried her HARDEST at science,

but Darren won the Science Cup.

"It's not fair!" sobbed the Little Princess. "I've tried my very hardest, but I haven't won anything!"

When all the big cups had been taken from the shelf . . .

. . . there was just one little one left that nobody had noticed.

But it turned out to be the best cup of all, because it was for . . .

. . . TRYING THE HARDEST, and because she *had* tried so hard, the Little Princess won it fair and square!

Other Little Princess Books

I Want My Potty!

I Want My Dinner!

I Want My Light On!

I Want My Present!

I Want a Friend!

I Want a Sister!

I Want to Go Home!

I Want Two Birthdays!

I Want a Party!

I Want to Do it By Myself!

I Want my Dummy!

I Don't Want to Wash My Hands!

I Don't Want to Go to Hospital!

LITTLE PRINCESS TV TIE-INS

Can I Keep It?

I Want My New Shoes!

I Don't Want a Cold!

I Want My Tent!

Fun in the Sun!

I Want to Do Magic!

I Want a Trumpet!

I Want My Sledge!

I Don't Like Salad!

I Don't Want to Comb My Hair!

I Want a Shop!

I Want to Go to the Fair!

I Want to Be a Cavegirl!

I Want to Be a Pirate!

I Want to Be Tall!

I Want My Puppets!

I Want My Sledge! Book and DVD